P9-BYE-953

# Billy and the Magic String

By Susan Karnovsky • Illustrated by Chris Demarest

WHISTLESTOP

Troll Associates

Developed by Nancy Hall, Inc.

Copyright © 1994 by Nancy Hall, Inc.
Text copyright ©1994 by Susan Karnovsky. Illustrations copyright © 1994 by Chris Demarest.
Published by Troll Associates, Inc. WhistleStop is a trademark of Troll Associates.
All rights reserved. No part of this book may be reproduced or utilized in any form or by any means,
electronic or mechanical, including photocopying, recording,
or by any information storage and retrieval system,
without written permission from the publisher.

Printed in the United States of America, bound in Mexico.
10 9 8 7 6 5 4 3 2 1

Billy found a piece of string. It wasn't tied to anything.

This string was very **long** and **strong.**
Its color was bright blue.

And when he tried to pick it up,
Bill found it didn't want him to.

It jumped way high up off the ground.

It dipped into a grin.

When Billy smiled and laughed aloud,
The string ha-ha'ed right back at him.

It twirled and swirled and spun around,
Then wound up in a ball.

It flipped right into Billy's hand
And made no fuss at all.

Then—**WOW**—that string jumped from his hand
Straight into Billy's pocket.

And then a little tip peeked out . . .

And shot off like a rocket.

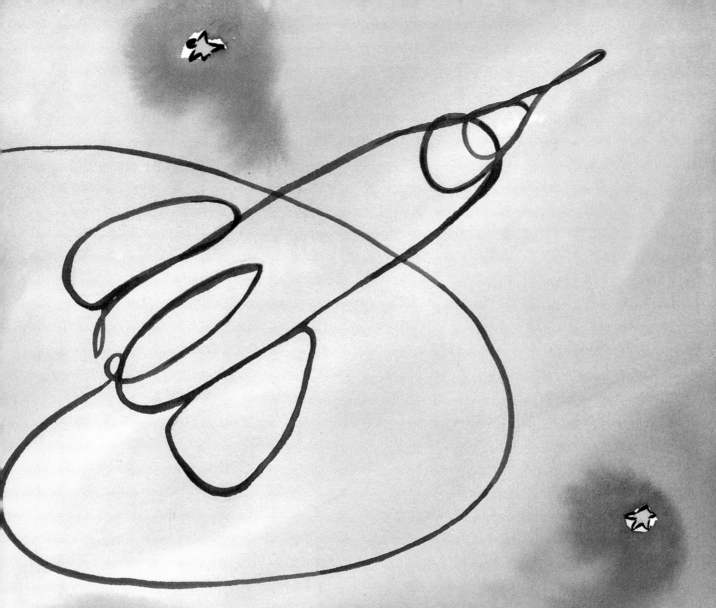

Billy held on with all his might.
They flew into the sky.

The string began to twist itself.

It turned into a **Y**.

Bill climbed inside the loop it made
And swung from side to side.

"Come live with me," Bill begged the string.
"Oh, no," the string replied.

"I won't tie kites to people.
I won't give yo-yos rides.

"I won't keep shoes on someone's feet,
And I won't keep boxes tied.

"I'd rather hop and skip and jump!

Let's go!" the string pulled Bill.

"But String," cried Bill.  "It's getting late."
"There's time," cried String, "for one more thrill."

The string went zippedy zigzag
And zoomed off in the sky.

Bill called out, "Please, String, wait for me."
But it was gone with no good-bye.

Bill shivered. "Oh, I miss my friend.
I'm cold and I'm afraid."
Then something tapped him on the arm.
"I'm back! Look what I've made!"

"You're here!" cried Bill. "I missed you so.
I can't believe my eyes!"

The string had made itself into
A sweater just Bill's size.

"Oh, String, look what you did for me."
Billy was warm that night.
"A friend like you is hard to find.
You're not too loose, and not too tight."

"Oh, thank you, String," Bill hugged his friend.
"But then you won't be free.
I know you need to be yourself—
And that's how you should be.

"I love you, String," Bill told his friend.
"You love me, Bill? You do?
Then maybe I will stay this way.
Because I love you, too."